Anthony

Clifford THE BIG RED DOG®

The Missing Beach Ball

by Sonali Fry

Illustrated by Mark Marderosian

Based on the Scholastic book series
"Clifford The Big Red Dog"
by Norman Bridwell

Cartwheel
·B·O·O·K·S·®

SCHOLASTIC INC.

New York   Toronto   London   Auckland   Sydney   Mexico City
New Delhi   Hong Kong   Buenos Aires

Visit Clifford at scholastic.com/clifford

Copyright © 2002 Scholastic Entertainment Inc.
All rights reserved. Based on the CLIFFORD THE BIG RED DOG book series
published by Scholastic Inc. ™ & © Norman Bridwell.
SCHOLASTIC, CARTWHEEL BOOKS, and associated logos are trademarks
and/or registered trademarks of Scholastic Inc.
CLIFFORD, CLIFFORD THE BIG RED DOG, and associated logos are trademarks
and/or registered trademarks of Norman Bridwell.

10 9 8 7 6 5 4 3 2   02 03 04 05 06

Printed in China
First printing, May 2002

It was a hot, sunny day on Birdwell Island.
Clifford was excited:
He was going to the beach!
Clifford found his toy. . . .

And then he went to Cleo's house.
"Hi, Cleo!" said Clifford. "Are you
ready to go to the beach?"
"I sure am!" said Cleo. "I'm going
to make the best sandcastle ever!"
"Great!" said Clifford. "Where's T-Bone?"

Just then, something
rolled in front of them.
It was a shiny beach ball!

"Hey, guys!" said T-Bone, running over.

"Check out my new beach ball. Isn't it great?"

"It sure is, T-Bone," said Clifford.

"We're going to have so much fun with it at the beach!" said T-Bone.

So, together, the dogs went to the beach.
When they got there, T-Bone and Clifford
played with T-Bone's new beach ball while
Cleo made a sandcastle.

The dogs were having fun when a big wave suddenly hit the shore.

Splash!

Clifford, Cleo, and T-Bone were soaked!

"Whoa!" yelled Cleo. "My sandcastle is ruined!"

"That's okay, Cleo," said T-Bone. "You can play with us. We're having so much fun with . . . hey—where's my beach ball?"

T-Bone's beach ball was gone!

Clifford, Cleo, and T-Bone sniffed around the sand.
"The wave must have washed it away," said Cleo.
"Don't worry, T. If we all work together, I'm sure
we can find it," said Clifford.

The three friends began to search for T-Bone's missing beach ball.
T-Bone looked under some seashells.
He found a bright red crab . . . but he didn't find his beach ball.

Cleo looked around some rocks.
She found a pink starfish... but she
didn't find T-Bone's beach ball.

Clifford decided to take a look underwater.
He saw lots of colorful coral, pretty shells,
and friendly sea creatures . . .
but he didn't see T-Bone's beach ball.

T-Bone was very sad. Where was his beach ball?
Suddenly, Clifford saw something bobbing in
the water.
"Look!" he yelled.
"It's my beach ball!" said T-Bone.

With Cleo and T-Bone on his back,
Clifford swam toward the beach ball.
But as they got closer, the beach ball got
farther and farther away.
"Hmmm... I think I need to go a little
faster," said Clifford. "Hang on, guys!"

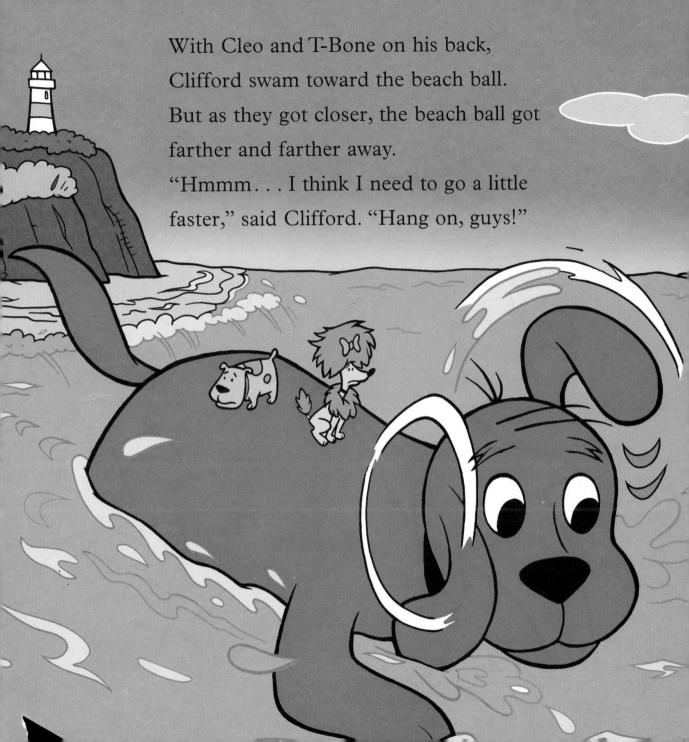

When the dogs caught up to the beach ball, they finally understood why it kept moving: A group of dolphins was playing with it! "Wow!" said Clifford. "They're having lots of fun with your beach ball."

While the dogs were watching, one of the dolphins hit the beach ball to T-Bone. T-Bone looked at the dolphins. They were bobbing up and down and making squawking noises. They were trying to talk to him!

T-Bone didn't know what to do.

"What are they saying?" he asked.

"Maybe they're telling us to leave them alone,"
said Cleo.

Clifford thought for a moment.
"I think they just want you to throw
the ball back to them, T," he said.
So that's what T-Bone did.

Then one of the dolphins hit
the ball to Clifford.
Clifford hit it back!

"Pass it to me!" Cleo called.

Again and again, the
dogs and the dolphins
passed the ball to
each other.

Soon, it was time for Clifford, T-Bone,
and Cleo to go home.
T-Bone looked at the dolphins, who were
happily playing with the beach ball.
"I think I'll let them keep my beach
ball," he said.

"Keep it? But it's your new toy!" said Cleo.

"I know," said T-Bone, "but look how happy they are.
I have lots of other toys that I can play with.
I want them to have this one."

The dolphins leaped from the water.

"I think they're saying 'thank you,'" said Clifford.

"You're welcome!" said T-Bone, waving to the dolphins.

So Clifford, T-Bone, and Cleo headed back to Birdwell Island, and the happy dolphins disappeared into the sunset.